Weekly Reader Children's Book Club Presents

CAPS FOR SALE

A Tale of a Peddler, Some Monkeys and Their Monkey Business

Told and Illustrated by

Esphyr Slobodkina

This book is a presentation of Newfield Publications, Inc. Newfield Publications offers book clubs for children from preschool through high school. For further information write to: **Newfield Publications, Inc.,** 4343 Equity Drive, Columbus, Ohio 43228.

Published by arrangement with Addison-Wesley Publishing Company, Inc. Newfield Publications is a federally registered trademark of Newfield Publications, Inc. Weekly Reader is a federally registered trademark of Weekly Reader Corporation.

1995 edition

READING RAINBOW® is a registered trademark of GPN/WNED-TV.

Young Scott Books

Once there was a peddler who sold caps. But he was not like an ordinary peddler carrying his wares on his back. He carried them on top of his head.

First he had on his own checked cap, then a bunch of gray caps, then a bunch of brown caps, then a bunch of blue caps, and on the very top a bunch of red caps.

He walked up and down the streets, holding himself very straight so as not to upset his caps.

As he went along he called, "Caps! Caps for sale! Fifty cents a cap!"

One morning he couldn't sell any caps. He walked up the street and he walked down the street calling, "Caps! Caps for sale. Fifty cents a cap."

But nobody wanted any caps that morning. Nobody wanted even a red cap.

He began to feel very hungry, but he had no money for lunch.

"I think I'll go for a walk in the country," said he. And he walked out of town — slowly, slowly, so as not to upset his caps.

He walked for a long time until he came to a great big tree.

"That's a nice place for a rest," thought he.

And he sat down very slowly under the tree and leaned back little by little against the tree-trunk so as not to disturb the caps on his head.

Then he put up his hand to feel if they were straight — first his own checked cap, then the gray caps, then the brown caps, then the blue caps, then the red caps on the very top.

They were all there.

So he went to sleep.

He slept for a long time.

When he woke up he was refreshed and rested.

But before standing up he felt with his hand to make sure his caps were in the right place.

All he felt was his own checked cap!

He looked to the right of him.
No caps.

He looked to the left of him.
No caps.

He looked in back of him.
No caps.

He looked behind the tree.
No caps.

Then he looked up into the tree.

And what do you think he saw?

On every branch sat a monkey. On every monkey

was a gray, or a brown, or a blue, or a red cap!

The peddler looked at the monkeys.

The monkeys looked at the peddler.

He didn't know what to do.

Finally he spoke to them.

"You monkeys, you," he said, shaking a finger at them, "you give me back my caps."

But the monkeys only shook their fingers back at him and said, "Tsz, tsz, tsz."

This made the peddler angry, so he shook both hands at them and said, "You monkeys, you! You give me back my caps."

But the monkeys only shook both their hands back at him and said, "Tsz, tsz, tsz."

Now he felt quite angry. He stamped his foot, and he said, "You monkeys, you! You better give me back my caps!"

But the monkeys only stamped their feet back at him and said, "Tsz, tsz, tsz."

By this time the peddler was really very, very angry. He stamped both his feet and shouted, "You monkeys, you! You must give me back my caps!"

But the monkeys only stamped both their feet back at him and said, "Tsz, tsz, tsz."

At last he became so angry that he pulled off his own cap, threw it on the ground, and began to walk away.

But then, each monkey pulled off his cap . . .

and all the gray caps,

and all the brown caps,

and all the blue caps,

and all the red caps came flying down

out of the tree.

So the peddler picked up his caps and put
them back on his head —

first his own checked cap,

then the gray caps,

then the brown caps,

then the blue caps,

then the red caps on the very top.

And slowly, slowly, he walked back to town calling, "Caps! Caps for sale! Fifty cents a cap!"